THE BIRD WAS THIRSTY

KNOWLEDGE BOOKS

MASTERY DECODABLES

The bird had a big trip.

The trip was long.

The trip was hot.

There was a lot of mud.

There was no water to sip.

The bird had no lip to sip water.

The bird has a beak.

The bird can gulp water.

Tas saw the bird was thirsty.

Tas ran to her water.

The bird went to the water.

The bird did not sip the water.

TAS

The bird had a big gulp of water.

The beak is a big cup.

The beak can trap water.

Tas is happy to get water for the bird.

The bird can talk.

Tas can hear the bird talk.

The bird can say wet, lip, sip.

Tas and the bird are happy.